DIARY OF A MINECRAFT ZOMBIE

BOOK 15

ATTACK OF THE GNOMES

DIARY OF A MINECRAFT ZOMBIE

BOOK 15

ATTACK OF THE GNOMES

BY

Zack Zombie

SATURDAY

"What is that?"

"I don't know."

"It looks like a troll."

"Maybe it's a baby villager."

"Baby villagers don't have
BEARDS. . .do they?"

"Who knows. Villagers are weird."

We all tried to figure out who the
small, creepy looking bearded guy in
front of the witch's house was.

"What's he doing?"

"It looks like he's gardening."

"I don't know. I've never seen anybody garden like that."

"Well, whatever they are, I think they're **SPREADING,**" Skelly said.

Skelly was right. Lately, these creepy looking bearded guys. . .or girls. . .have been showing up all over the place.

It's like they just popped out of the ground overnight.

All I can say is that they creep me out.

Especially when they stare at me with their beady little eyes.

It's like, no matter where I move, they just keep looking at me.

EYEBALLS...So wrong.

☀ SUNDAY

Today I was thinking about all the crazy stuff that's happened to me the past few months.

It kinda made me **WONDER** if there is something wrong with me.

Like, is it just me?

Or is this much drama just part of being a Zombie pre-teen kid?

I mean, I don't get it.

That kid Gabe, down the street, doesn't have a lot of stuff going on in his life.

I mean, yeah, he's a noob.

But his life is pretty normal.

Or that other kid, Francis, who lives next door.

He's a Zombie. And he's my age.

But you don't see him having crazy drama in his life.

I just wish that I could live a normal, DRAMA-FREE life like those guys.

Now that I think of it, that's exactly what I'm going to do.

From now on, my number one rule is going to be. . .

'NO DRAMA.'

That means no matter what happens,
if it looks like drama, or even smells
like drama, I don't want it.

Even if all of Minecraft is going to be
destroyed, I'm not getting involved.

I'm just going to scare villagers,
eat boogers, raise crops, and live a
NORMAL Minecraft Zombie life.

Urrrrrggghhhh!

Look at me, I'm a normal, boring
Zombie. . .

Urrrrrggghhhh!

M✺NDAY

"Hi, I'm Cassie, I just transferred in from another school," the girl next to Alex said.

"Oh. . .uh. . .hi?" Skelly said, stuttering.

"Hi, I'm Slimey," Slimey said right before he **BURST** into a bunch of little pieces.

"Hsssssss," was all Creepy said.

Yeah, I don't think these guys are used to talking to girls.

Especially not human ones.

"WHAT'S THAT?!!!" Creepy yelled.

"Oh, that's Oslow," Cassie said. "He's my cat. Say hello, Oslow."

MEOOWWWWWWW.

Hsssss. PLOP!

"EEEWWWWWWWWW."

"Sorry," Creepy said. "Cats just make me **NERVOUS**, thasss all."

"Hey, Cassie. I'm Zack. But you can call me Zombie."

"Hi, Zombie," Cassie said as she picked up Oslow.

"Me and Cassie are going back to our village now," Alex said. "Just see if you can help Slimey. And while you're at it, tell Skelly to wipe the **DROOL** off his chin."

As they were walking away, I could hear Alex say, "Man, even mob boys are weird."

It was really good seeing Alex, though.

What's really cool is that Alex and Cassie are going to be in our school this semester.

It's part of a Villager and Mob Scare school, **FOREIGN EXCHANGE** program.

Now, the program has been going on for a few months. But there haven't been any kids brave enough to be part of it.

That was because the first kid that tried it was a Creeper named Harold.

He thought it would be fun to go to school with Villagers.

But somebody forgot to tell the Villager school that Harold was a Creeper.

First day there, somebody thought it was a good idea to give Harold a high-five.

Totally **RUINED** it for the rest of us.

. . .and for Harold.

But it's going to be fun having Alex around.

Yeah, she's no drama at all.

Hmm. But, I wonder what Cassie's all about. . .

TUESDAY

Well, so far, my life has been as normal and boring as ever.

It's kind of weird, actually.

Usually, I'd hear about a **GIANT METEOR** about to destroy our planet or a huge volcano about to explode in my backyard.

Or I'd hear about some aliens that had infiltrated our village and replaced all my friends with life-sized synthetic robots.

Or there would be some Mojang update that would totally make Minecraft PVP the lamest ever.

But, you know, I'm not complaining.

I'm just happy that my life is **DRAMA-FREE.**

KRESH!

Ow!

What was that?

Oh, man. I totally wasn't looking where I was going. I hope the witch is not upset that I broke her creepy little troll statue.

Suddenly, the **WITCH** came out and gave me a weird look.

Next thing I know, she started waving her arms around like a crazy lady.

Oh man, what now?

"Double, double toil and trouble,

Fire burn and cauldron bubble."

Now what is she doing in front of that cauldron?

"Fillet of a fenny snake,

In the cauldron boil and bake."

Huh?

"Eye of newt and toe of frog,

Wool of bat and tongue of dog."

Nasty.

"Adder's fork and foot of duck,

Bring this Zombie all **BAD LUCK.**"

Wait. . .what did she just say?

Next thing I know, I felt tingly all over.

Then the little hairy troll's head rolled across the grass and got back on his body.

Oh, it was just a spell to fix the **CREEPY MAN DOLL.**

Well, I guess I'm okay.

Whew!. . .That was close.

WEDNESDAY

Just when I thought my life was getting back to normal. . .

"Isn't he adorable?"

"He sure looks deep in thought," my dad said.

"Mama, it's a bunny," my little brother said.

"He's not a bunny, honey, he's a **GNOME,** my mom said. "A lot of our neighbors are getting them these days. People say they bring good luck."

Of course, my mom was talking about the creepy little troll thing that she brought into our house.

My mom said she was at the market today and when she saw it, she just couldn't **RESIST** bringing it home.

Yeah, right.

Something tells me it's probably all part of the **CURSE** the witch decided to drop on me yesterday.

"I think I will call him, Laslow," my mom said. "And he's going to bring us good luck."

Yeah, I think I'm going to need it.

My mom decided to put it in
the garden right outside MY
WINDOW.

Just what I need. . .

A creepy old man looking through my
window.

So wrong.

☀ THURSDAY ☀

Boink!

"Ow!"

I woke up this morning when my
IRON SWORD fell off the wall
and hit me on the
head.

"Zombie, what's going
on up there?"

"Nothing, Mom," I yelled.

That's weird, I thought. That's never
happened before.

I looked in the mirror, and I had the sword sticking out of my forehead.

Oh man, I can't go to school like this.

It took a few minutes, but I finally got it out.

The hard part was massaging my head back into **SHAPE.**

I think I got it, but I'm not sure.

After looking at the time, I saw I was late.

So I grabbed my books and ran down the stairs.

"Whoa!"

BUMP!

BAP!

BUNK!

BUHP!

BLAM!

"Zombie, what is the matter? You seem **CLUMSIER** than usual this morning."

"I don't know, Mom," I said as she handed me my arms.

"Maybe we need to take you to the doctor," she said.

Oh, man, not the doctor.

I hate going to the doctor.

Not only does he have really bad breath. . .

Blech!

But he has a big, ugly mole on his nose.

It's huge.

One time, when the doctor was **EXAMINING** me, he accidentally touched me with his mole.

It felt like a big hairy pimple.

. . .And it was oily.

Blech!

But the thing that really bothers me is **TAKING OFF** my skin in front of a total stranger.

So embarrassing.

And there's always a draft. . .

"I'm okay, Mom, just a little tired. . . that's all."

As I was putting my legs back on, I noticed my SKATEBOARD on the floor next to my feet.

How did that get there? I thought.

Man, there are some really strange things going on around here.

FRIDAY

At school today, all the kids were talking about all the creepy gnomes that started **POPPING UP** all over the neighborhood.

"My mom got one, and it looks like its fishing," Slimey said.

"My dad got one, and it looks like its **SURFING,**" Skelly said.

"We got one that throws up **RAINBOWS,**" Creepy said.

Whoa, cool!

"It's kinda weird how they just started popping up all over the place, right?" Creepy asked.

"I heard that it all started when the Red Pumpkin commercial came out," Skelly said.

"What Red Pumpkin commercial?" I asked.

"You haven't seen it?" Creepy said. "Man, that Red Pumpkin guy really creeps me out. Hsssss."

"Whoa, calm down, dude," I said. "It's only a commercial. It can't be that scary."

All the guys just looked at me with a scared look on their face.

"Seriously. How **SCARY** could it be?"

Later, after dinner, I was in the living room when my dad turned on the TV News.

"And for today's top story: some Minecraft mobs have gone missing in town. They were last seen a few days ago working on their lawns, but they have suddenly and mysteriously disappeared without a trace. Some say that

aliens have come down to find more specimens. Or some believe that a charged Creeper decided to go for a stroll. But, if you have any information regarding the missing individuals, please contact us at 555-MOBS. More on this story tonight at 11."

"Well, that's weird," my mom said. "I wonder if its anyone we know."

"I'm sure there is a REASONABLE explanation for it," my dad said. "Maybe they all won tickets to MineCon. You know, I've always wanted to go."

All of sudden, the weirdest commercial came on the TV.

Gnomes, Gnomes. . .Get your gnomes, get your gnomes, get your gnomes.

Gnomes, Gnomes. . .Get your gnomes at the Red Pumpkin!

Get your Gnome and get good luck, get good luck, get good luck.

Get your Gnome and get good luck at the Red Pumpkin!

What the...?

Then the creepiest looking guy came on the TV. He had a giant red pumpkin on his head, a black cape and long bony fingers. And with his claw hands, he was stroking a cat.

Then he spoke in the most blood-curdling voice. . .

"If you want good luck, answered wishes, and to see your dreams come true, then come down to the Red Pumpkin Emporium and get your lucky gnome today!"

Gnomes, Gnomes...Get your gnomes, get your gnomes, get your gnomes.

Gnomes, Gnomes. . .Get your gnomes at the Red Pumpkin!

What the crazy, what?

Man, the guys weren't kidding. That was one of the most **DISTURBING** commercials I'd ever seen.

Especially that Red Pumpkin guy.

That guy looks like he belongs in a horror movie that's rated 'F' for **FREAKY.**

And what's up with that weird cat?

Then my dad got up to go to the kitchen to help my mom.

But, seriously, that commercial freaked me out really bad.

So, I grabbed the remote to turn off the TV.

Click.

BOOM!

"WHAT WAS THAT?!!" my mom yelled, running in from the kitchen.

She couldn't see much because of all the **SMOKE.**

"Zombie, where are you?"

"Mrphfrmphth!" I said.

After the smoke cleared, it took my mom and dad a few minutes to find the rest of my body parts.

"Mrphfrmphth!!" I said as my dad pried my head out of the wall.

POP!

"There you go. Well, I guess having a hard head comes in handy, hee hee," my dad said.

"What happened?" I said as my dad handed me my dismembered hand, still clutching the remote control.

"I don't know. Something must've caused a **POWER SURGE** in the TV," my dad said.

"That's odd," my mom said. "We just got that TV."

Oh, man! I bet it's the witch's curse!

The hex she put on me is already bringing me all sorts of bad luck.

I need to do something fast before
this thing kills me. . .

. . .or seriously damages my **SOCIAL**
LIFE.

But what can I do?

What can I do?

SATURDAY

I went to go see Steve today to see if he could help me get rid of the witch's curse.

I can always count on Steve. He knows everything.

Well, not about anything **IMPORTANT.**

More like, if it's crazy, outrageous or totally bonkers, Steve totally knows about it.

"Hey, Steve."

"Well look what the cat dragged in," Steve said.

"Oh, man, not again!" I said.

I started looking around to see if I could find the cat.

That's because cats really like **ZOMBIE FLESH.**

So you have to be real careful when there are cats around.

Especially when you need to pee. . .

I mean...it's really hard to do stuff when you don't have fingers..

"Dude, what are you looking for?" Steve asked me.

"Nothing. Just forget it."

"Ooookay. Anyway, so, Zombie, what's up?"

"Dude, I need to know how to get rid of a curse!" I said.

"A curse, huh? Yeah, those are really tough to get rid of," Steve said. "What kind of curse was it?"

"I don't know. All I know is that I have been having the **WORST LUCK** these past few days."

"Uh, oh, a bad luck curse. Those are the worst," Steve said. "I remember getting one of those once. Talk about drama."

That was not what I wanted to hear.

"Well, can you help me get rid of it?"

"Usually a bad luck curse can only be stopped by some kind of **GOOD LUCK CHARM,**" Steve said.

"What's that?"

"A good luck charm is an object that has been infused with magic by undergoing some type of supernatural ritual," Steve said. "Like an Ender Pearl."

"What's an Ender Pearl?"

"Well, an Ender Pearl is a special magical stone that brings good luck to its owner," Steve said. "It's what helped me get over my curse."

"So where can I get one?"

"Well, they're not easy to get. You have to get one from an Enderman."

"Oh, that's easy. I'll just get one from this Enderman kid in my class named Franklin."

"Uh. . .well, it's not that simple. You see, **ENDER PEARLS** come from Endermen," Steve said, making weird gestures with his hands.

"Huh?"

"You know. . .from an Enderman. . ." Steve said again while making more funny gestures with his hands.

"Hmm?"

"All right, you get Ender Pearls from Enderman poop, okay?" Steve said.

"Wait. . .what?"

"Yeah, you're going to have to get a **LITTLE DIRTY** if you want to get your hands on an Ender Pearl. Up to your elbows."

"Ewwwww. Seriously?"

"Yep. And you can't just ask for it either. Endermen are really shy when it comes to their bodily functions. So, they'll never talk about it," Steve said. "You're going to have to take it."

What?!

Man, I did not like the sound of that.

But I knew if I didn't get something to help me get rid of this curse, my life was going to full of a lot of drama. . .

Or really big **EXPLOSIONS.**

So I called Franklin and asked him if I could come over.

Ding, Dong!

"Hey, Zombie?" Franklin said. "I was really happy when you called. I don't have a lot of friends, so I was really excited when said you wanted to hang out."

Yeah, Franklin doesn't have a lot of friends because he's kinda, you know. . .weird.

It's just that he does some really freaky stuff, which kinda makes him a **BIG TARGET** for the kids at school.

Like, one day he started eating brownie rolls in swim class.

What made it weird is that no one had ever seen a **BROWNIE ROLL,** until that day.

So watching Franklin eat brown rolls while in the pool had a really weird effect on the other kids.

I heard the other kids couldn't stop projectile vomiting on each other.

Like I said. . .weird.

"What would you like to play?" Franklin asked me. "I know all kind of games. But my favorite is, 'Find my Belly Button.'"

Wait. . .what?

"Uh. . .can I use your bathroom first?"
I asked him.

"Sure, it's right over there."

After my bathroom break, I had to
find a way to get an Ender Pearl from
Franklin.

So, I convinced him to have an
EATING CONTEST.

His mom just baked a whole bunch of
brownie rolls, too.

Figures.

So we went at it for like an hour.

I thought for sure that Franklin would have to go to the bathroom after eating all those brownie rolls.

But he just kept chugging them like they were candy.

So I tried adding some **HOT SPICES** to his food.

Spicy food always makes my butt sneeze, so I was sure they would do the trick.

But Franklin just inhaled his food like a vacuum cleaner.

Man, no wonder I couldn't find his belly button.

All of a sudden, halfway through our eating contest I heard. . .

"FRANLKINI!"

It was Franklin's dad.

"Who put a Ziploc **STORAGE BAG** in the toilet?!!"

Oh, man. I was sure the jig was up. My Ender Pearl catcher was discovered.

"Well, the toilet's all backed up now," Franklin's dad said. "There's poop everywhere. Now who's going to help me clean up this mess?"

"I'll be happy to help," I said.

Ender Pearl, here I come.

After an hour of helping clean up, I think Franklin's dad figured it was time for me to go home.

I think he might have gotten weirded out when I started swimming in Ender poo.

Or when I started putting it in my pockets.

Or when I started making poo angels.

And it really didn't help that Franklin kept yelling, "Marco!"

After I got home, I was totally BUMMED I didn't find an Ender Pearl.

So I called Steve to let him know what happened.

"Oh, yeah," Steve said.

"About that. . ."

SUNDAY

Yesterday, I was totally up to my elbows in Endermen poo.

All because I totally forgot that Steve loves to play **PRACTICAL JOKES.**

Yeah, he got me good.

I wanted to get him back, but he just went out of town for a few days.

Yeah, you'd better run.

But, I'm back at square one.

Like, how am I supposed to get rid of this bad luck curse now?

As I was thinking about it, I bumped into old man Jenkins on the street.

He told me that all I needed to do to ward off bad luck was to hang a **RABBIT'S FOOT** around my neck.

I know it sounded kind of nasty, but I needed all the help I could get.

So, I found a cute little bunny in the forest. . .

. . .And now I'm carrying around a rabbit's foot around my neck.

It's really **ITCHY**, though.

I just wished old man Jenkins told me how to keep the rabbit from moving around so much.

MNDAY

I got a lot of weird looks at school today.

Well you know, more than I usually do.

I think it was because of the rabbit's foot around my neck.

I don't get what the big deal is. It's not like he's moving around anymore.

And I only had to use a few **STAPLES**. . .

But that was the least of my worries.

I still had a witch's death curse hanging over my head, which could strike at any moment.

So I did everything I could to stay away from anything **DANGEROUS.**

Like, I totally stayed out of the boy's bathroom.

Which is like the most dangerous place in school.

Especially when there are Minecraft kids around.

Like, the other day, a Wither kid came down with a bad case of the runs.

And it didn't help he had three heads.

Or three butts.

Man. . .talk about explosive diarrhea.

M*NDAY
LATER THAT* NIGHT. . .

After dinner today, the weirdest stuff happened.

First, when I was getting ready for bed, I thought I heard something.

It sounded like **LITTLE FEET** running around in my room.

Then, when I was brushing my teeth, I thought I saw a shadow behind me.

I was really getting spooked.

Oh, yeah, by the way, I started brushing my teeth a few weeks ago.

I know I only have a few, but I wanted them to look nice.

So, my mom bought me a new Zombie **TOOTHPASTE.**

It gets my teeth a nice yellowish brown, which makes me look real manly.

And it's supposed to attract maggots, which is always good.

Comes in handy when I get hungry in the middle of the night.

So after I finished brushing my teeth, I laid down.

But then, I thought I heard something under my bed.

So, of course, by now, I was totally freaked out.

I thought maybe I should look under my bed. But knowing my luck, there's probably a **CLOWN** down there, ready to rip my face off.

Man, I really hate clowns.

So, I decided to be strong and look under the bed to see what it was.

Yeah, I know, you should never do that.

Like in the movies, I always yell at the dumb kid when he decides to check **UNDER THE BED.**

But I couldn't help it.

I think stupidity comes with puberty, so I'm not responsible for my actions.

So then, I slowly started to peek under the bed.

And I took my time too.

I'm going to make that creepy clown fight for his lunch, I thought.

Just a little more, and I could see what was under there.

Just a little more. . .

Just a little more. . .

RRRRAAAWWWRRRR!!!!

TUESDAY

Psyche!

Oh, sorry.

I forgot to tell you that I like to play practical jokes too.

I hope you didn't pee your pants or anything.

Anyway, I couldn't find whatever was causing those **WEIRD NOISES** in my room last night.

It was just too weird and creepy.

But, my mom's toothpaste worked like a charm.

Best midnight snack, ever.

My bad luck hasn't changed, though.

Like when I was walking to school this morning, I got splashed and covered in this blue liquid.

I didn't even know where it came from.

All I remember was an **AIRPLANE** flew over my head, which I thought was really cool.

And next thing I know, I'm covered in blue juice.

Man, that stuff was really hard to get off my clothes.

And out of my mouth.

. . .Especially the **CHUNKS.**

But today we had school field trip, which I was totally psyched about.

"Hey, Ms. Bones, where are we going today?" one kid asked.

"We're going to the Minecraft Geological Museum," Ms. Bones said. "It's supposed to have all rarest gems from all around Minecraft."

"Whoa!"

"Ms. Bones, do they have **DIAMONDS?**" another kid asked.

"Yes."

"Do they have Redstone?"

"Yes."

"Do they have
Lapis Lazuli?"

"Yes."

"I like her.
She's purty."

"Wait. . .what?"

"Do they have EMERALDS?"

"Actually, they have the largest
Emerald in all of Minecraft."

"Whoa!"

Yeah, this is trip is going to be so cool.

TUESDAY
LATER THAT DAY...

At the museum, we saw all kinds of gems from all of Minecraft.

They had every gem you could ever imagine.

But the coolest part of the trip was the **GIANT EMERALD** exhibit.

When we walked in, it was awesome.

There was a giant Emerald that was so big, it was bigger than me and Skelly standing on top of each other.

There was a Zombie **GEOLOGIST** there that was giving us the tour. She taught us everything about the Emerald we wanted to know.

"Where did it come from?" Skelly asked.

"This marvelous specimen was deep within the earth until one day it was spit up into the air when a giant **VOLCANO** erupted 600 million years ago."

"Whoa!"

"Who found it?" Alex asked.

"Actually, it was a joint expedition between the Minecraft world and the human world. As a matter of fact, the giant Emerald has two parts. This is only one of them."

"Where's the other part?"

"The humans have the other part," the geologists said. "It was said that if the two parts came together, they would be too powerful to control. So we decided to keep one and let the HUMANS keep one far away in the human world."

"Whoa!"

"How powerful are they?" Cassie asked

"Well," the geologist continued. "They are said to be so powerful that together they can control the minds of any Minecraft

Mobs that comes close to it. That is why this Emerald is also known in some circles as the Mind Emerald."

"Whoa!"

Yeah, this trip was really off the hook.

WEDNESDAY

Today I had to write an **ESSAY** for homework about our field trip yesterday.

Ms. Bones said that the essay had to be five hundred words.

The only problem is that I don't know **FIVE HUNDRED** words.

Man, I don't think I even know a hundred words.

But there are words that I really like.

Words like. . .

Cake!

Or booger.

Or nose maggot.

I don't know why, but those words just make me feel tingly all over.

Now, there are probably words that a Zombie should never say.

I guess it's because they sound so **WEIRD.**

Words like. . .

Brains.

Or entrails.

Or ears.

Ewwww. So nasty.

Then there are words that just make no sense. Words like. . .

Tinkle.

I mean, I don't get it.

Whenever I go pee, I don't hear any bells.

Although, my ears were **RINGING** when that Wither kid had the runs the other day.

Talk about a dishonorable discharge.

Anyway, I've got to start writing this essay or I'll get a big fat F in my class.

The only problem is that I tend to procraftinate.

Yeah, I think school might be totally lost on me.

* THURSDAY *

I woke up this morning, and I was
TOTALLY LATE for school!

I don't know what happened.

I sat down to write my essay, and
next thing I know I woke up this
morning and I was late.

Yeah, I know I shouldn't have played
a few hours of video games.

And, yeah, I know I shouldn't have
spent a couple of hours watching cat
videos. . .

. . .or watching epic fail compilations.

. . .or watching the best Minecraft Memes ever.

So awesome.

But I had plenty of time to do my homework, really.

And it wasn't my fault somebody left a cup of **WARM MILK** by my bed.

But, next thing I know, I woke up this morning late for school.

Man, now I know I'm going to get a big fat F in my class!

What am I going to do?

☀ THURSDAY ☀
LATER THAT DAY. . .

Well, I didn't get an F in my class.

I guess my luck wasn't so bad after all.

I mean, the whole school did burn down.

But it wasn't **MY FAULT**, really.

I mean, all I did was walk into the Chemistry class to say hi to my friend Conrad.

How did I know that they were studying about TNT?

And, I guess it didn't help that Conrad was a Creeper.

FRIDAY

I saw Alex in school today.

She was in her Minecraft PVP Sword Fighting class.

"Hey, Alex."

"Hey, Zombie. Do you want to spar with me?" she said as she unsheathed her diamond sword.

"Oh, no no no no no. I'm a lover not a **FIGHTER.**"

"Come on, Zombie, you'll like it," she said, handing me a wooden sword.

Then she stood in front of me in her attack stance.

"Ready?"

"Uh. . .I guess so," I said.

All of a sudden, "Ahhhhhhhhhh!" Alex yelled as she lunged at me.

All I could do was SCREAM and close my eyes.

AAAAAAAH! PLOP!

"Uh. . .Zombie," Alex said.

"Yeah?" I asked with my eyes still closed.

"I think we'd better go to the nurse's office," she said.

"Huh?"

When I opened my eyes, all I could see when I looked up was Alex putting my body parts into her backpack.

After the **NURSE'S** office, Alex and I went to get lunch at the cafeteria.

"Hey, where's Cassie?" I asked Alex.

"I don't know," she said. "She's in two of my classes, but I didn't see her at all today. Actually, she's been **ABSENT** since the field trip."

"Yeah, humans can be weird sometimes."

Then Alex unsheathed her sword halfway and gave me her usual look.

But I was saved just in time by an announcement over the loudspeaker. . .

"Attention, students, we have a special announcement to make. The Red Pumpkin Emporium has decided to sponsor our Minecraft Scare School athletic program which we are very proud of. And we have decided to show our **APPRECIATION** for their generous contribution by showing their commercial every day during recess for the next few weeks. So, enjoy your lunch!"

Suddenly, that creepy commercial came on the TV in the cafeteria.

Gnomes, Gnomes. . .Get your gnomes, get your gnomes, get your gnomes.

Gnomes, Gnomes. . .Get your gnomes at the Red Pumpkin!

Get your Gnome and get good luck, get good luck, get good luck.

Get your Gnome and get good luck at the Red Pumpkin!

If you want good luck, answered wishes and to see your dreams come true, then come down to the Red Pumpkin Emporium and Get your lucky gnome today!

Gnomes, Gnomes. . .Get your gnomes, get your gnomes, get your gnomes.

Gnomes, Gnomes. . .Get your gnomes at the Red Pumpkin!

"Zombie. . .Zombie. . .ZOMBIE!"

"Urrrgghhhh. . .wuzzat?"

"Zombie, what happened to you?" Alex asked. "You just **ZONED OUT.**"

"Huh? Seriously?"

"Yeah, dude. You okay?"

"I don't know. I was just thinking about how cool it would be to get a gnome."

"You are so weird," Alex said.

Then I looked around and all the other mob kids were staring at the TV and drooling. Kinda like when a new Minecraft update comes out.

Now, what was really weird is that the only one that wasn't affected was Alex.

Man, things are getting so weird around here.

SATURDAY

Today I just spent the whole day at home, bored out of my skull.

I really hate when that happens.

Getting my **SKULL** back in can be a real pain sometimes.

Anyway, I was bored because I've been **BANNED** from playing video games and from watching TV.

My mom and dad said that they think I spend too much time in front of the screen.

Something about it being bad for my eyes.

Parents just don't make any sense sometimes.

So, I had to find something to do.

I tried reading a **BOOK.**

But it felt too much like school, so I put an end to that quick.

Then I tried to finish my new Minecraft Booger sculpture.

But after adding a few extra parts, I got low on snot so I gave it a break.

So, then I thought I could take a **NAP** to pass the time.

But when I was lying in bed, the weirdest thing happened.

I could **SWEAR** I heard a noise that sounded like little feet, again.

I thought it was my little brother playing tricks, but then I remembered he went out with my mom and dad.

Huh. Maybe the fumes from my sculpture are getting to me, I thought.

They say that kids can get sick from inhaling too much snot fumes.

So, I opened the window to get some fresh air.

But then I noticed something was missing.

Hey, where's that creepy little gnome statue? I thought.

Huh. Maybe mom finally realized how weird it was and got rid of it.

So, after putting my sculpture away, I turned around to close the window again.

WHAT THE WHAT!

When I looked outside again, there he was!

The creepy little gnome was back!

What is going on? I could swear that little troll wasn't there a little while ago.

Man, those snot fumes must've really gotten to me.

So I tried forgetting the whole thing, and I just took my nap.

"KRASH!"

Something hit me on the head and woke me up again.

Except this time, when I looked at the floor, it wasn't my iron sword. It was my booger sculpture, and it was broken into a thousand pieces.

What the what'n what is going on?!!

Pit, pat, pit, pat, pit, pat.

Then I heard those little feet again.

Man, either I'm going crazy or something is just not right around here.

PIT, PAT, PIT, PAT, PIT, PAT.

When I heard the feet again, I chased whatever it was out of my bedroom, down the stairs and out the back door.

I was sure I was going to catch him.

But when I got outside, there was nothing there.

Just the same old dirt and grass, and the creepy little gnome.

Except this time, I could swear I saw a creepy little smile on his face.

✷ SUNDAY ✷

Today, I got ready for bed.

I put away all my toys in the dresser drawers so they wouldn't hit me on the head.

I took all the pictures down off the wall too.

And I got rid of all **SHARP OBJECTS** and anything that could maim, chop or dismember.

Then I turned off the lights, went to bed, closed my eyes, and went to sleep.

Pit, pat, pit, pat, pit, pat.

Pit, pat, pit, pat, pit, pat.

Pit, pat, pit, pat. . .

"GOTHCHA!"

I grabbed the little creature and stuffed him into a potato sack.

He was **WRIGGLING** and moving around, and he even kicked me in the face.

But, I wasn't letting go.

I finally caught him, and I wanted some answers.

So, I grabbed some rope and tied the bag really good.

He kept moving around a lot, so I took the bag and I decided to practice some of my **WRESTLING** moves on it.

First, I did the Ultimate Warrior Gorilla Suplex Smash on him. . .

BOOM!

Then I followed it up with the Triple Threat, Galactic Pile Driver. . .

SLAM!

Then I climbed on my bed and finished with the Quadruple Rope Elbow Dropkick. . .

KAZOW!

Yeah. . . the SOUND EFFECTS made it so much better.

"Okay, I give up, I give up!" the little creature said.

So then I turned on the lights.

I undid the top of the **POTATO** sack, but I kept the little guy roped up.

"I give up, I give up. . .you caught me," he said.

"Aha! I knew it was you!"

"No more wrestling moves, please," he said, stunned by my magnificence.

"Okay. But I want answers, now," I said.

"Well, my name is Collywobbles the gnome, at your service," the little guy said.

"That's a funny name," I said, laughing.

"Oh yeah? What kind of name is Zombie? That's like calling somebody Dummy or Moron. So lame."

"Hey!" I said, getting on my bed for another Suplex Elbow Dropkick.

"I take it back! I take it back!" he said after I showed him who's **BOSS**.

"I guess you can call me Laslow," he said.

"So, Laslow, why are you here?"

"Well, I am a gnome, from a town called Snollygoster. It's a wonderful Gnome town where we spend all day having fun and living the good gnome life away from all you weird Minecraft mob people."

"Seriously?"

"Yes. Father Notch put us there, and he promised us that one day he would introduce us to the Minecraft world in the next Minecraft update. But, alas, Father Notch never came."

"Uh. . .I have some **BAD NEWS** for you, dude. . ."

"Anyway," the little gnome continued, "we have been living in relative peace until one day we were kidnapped by a weird creature with a really big head, shaped like a pumpkin."

"The Red Pumpkin!"

"Yes. And we have been his slaves since. You see, he uses his magic power to control us, and he makes us do bad things to all of the families that buy us and bring us home."

"Wait. . .what?"

"Yes, uh. . .sorry about the TV explosion thing, by the way," Laslow said.

"Wait. . .**THAT WAS YOU?!!!**"

"Yes, and I really felt really bad about your school burning down, too."

"You're kidding?"

"And the skateboard by the stairs. . .and your booger sculpture. . .and. . ."

"Wait, all that was you?!! And how about when I fell asleep and forgot my essay? That was you too?!!!"

"Uh. . .no, that was all you, buddy."

Figures.

Wow, all my bad luck. . .that was all Laslow.

"Well, what about the witch's curse?"

"Oh, you mean your neighbor Gladys? She's **HARMLESS.** Don't pay her no mind. She's just a few cards short of a full deck, that one."

"Whoa, it totally makes sense now," I said.

"So, what about those creepy commercials?" I continued. "What are those for?"

"The Red Pumpkin wants to get more and more families to buy gnomes so that on the next full moon, which is in a few days by the way, he's going to unleash all the gnomes to attack and **DESTROY** your whole village."

I had to ask.

"So how do we stop him?" I asked Laslow.

"Well, we need to **FREE** all my comrades from the Red Pumpkin's spell. But the only way is by finding the Red Pumpkin's lair.

"Where is it?"

"Well, if you loosen these ropes, I can show you a map that shows you exactly where the Red Pumpkin lives."

I wasn't sure if I could **TRUST** the little minion. Especially after finding out that he caused all the recent drama in my life.

But he looked harmless enough. Plus, I think the little guy knew who was boss.

So I loosened the ropes, and the little guy started reaching in his pockets.

Then he turned around and said, "Sucker!"

Pit, pat, pit, pat, pit, pat!

And he ran away!

Man, that's what I get for believing a creepy **LITTLE GNOME.**

So then I just brushed my teeth and got ready for bed.

And as I grabbed the potato sack from the floor, a **PICTURE** fell out.

I was hoping it was a picture of the map to the Red Pumpkin's hideout.

But, it wasn't a picture of a map.

It was just a picture of Laslow smiling. . .

. . .while he cleaned the toilet with my toothbrush.

M✺NDAY

I had a tough time convincing my Mom that Laslow was really **ALIVE** and that he ran away.

"No really, Mom," I said. "Laslow caused all these crazy things to happen, and he's the reason I've been having all this bad luck. And he's the reason I didn't finish my essay."

Yeah, she didn't buy it.

But, you can't blame a Zombie for trying.

Anyway, since the school burned down, we didn't have any school today.

But my mom and dad still had to go to a parent-teacher conference.

Something about bussing the kids to the Nether to finish off the semester.

I don't know if that's such a good idea, though.

Like, one time I gave a Zombie Pigman kid a **HIGH FIVE.** Next thing I know, all his friends ganged up on me.

Talk about a bunch of hotheads.

Anyway, I was home alone when I heard a familiar sound.

Pit, pat, pit, pat, pit, pat.

"Laslow! Is that you?"

"Hello, Zombie," Laslow said.

"What are you doing here?" I said as I got up on the bed to do my Elbow Dropkick on him.

"No, no, please. I need your help," he said.

"My help? For what? You already caused enough DRAMA in my life."

"Please, Zombie. The Red Pumpkin has all my people under his spell, and he is planning to release his fury on your village in the next few days."

"So what do you need my help for?" I asked him.

"I need your help to free my countrymen from the Red Pumpkin's spell."

I could tell Laslow was serious. But I just didn't know how much I could trust the **LITTLE RUNT**, though.

But if he was right, and the Red Pumpkin does unleash his fury, then it could totally wipe out our village.

Oh, man, here we go again.

"Okay, I'll help you," I said. "But, you owe me a new toothbrush."

Laslow just looked at me. . .and smiled.

M✳NDAY
LATER THAT✳
DAY. . .

Before we got to the Red Pumpkin's lair, we met up with a few more of Laslow's **FRIENDS.**

"Hi, my name is Bumfuzzle," one of the gnomes said.

"My name is Cattywampus," said another.

"And my name is Kerfuffle," the little one said.

"And my name is Gardlyoo," the girl one said.

Wow, and I thought I had a weird name.

They all seemed kinda nice, in a creepy bearded-troll kind of way.

Yeah, even the girl had a beard too.

The Red Pumpkin's lair was in a big cave. But, when we got there, it was guarded by some even **BIGGER GNOMES** than I had seen before.

At the entrance, there was a line of gnomes tied up in Minecarts. They were being led inside the cave, up a rock hill that led to a big altar on the top.

And, at the very top there was a giant green Emerald. And next to it was the

Red Pumpkin and his cat sitting on a throne next to it.

"Hey, that's the Mind Emerald!" I said because I recognized it from the museum.

So that's how the Red Pumpkin is controlling all the gnomes, I thought.

"So, what's the plan?" I asked.

"Well, you can't go in there looking like that," Laslow said. "You need a **DISGUISE.**"

Then the bearded girl handed me a costume.

"Here you go," she said. "We made it just for you."

It fit like a glove, which was kind of surprising.

"Don't forget the beard," the girl gnome said.

"So, how do I look?"

"Whew-wee! If you weren't a Zombie, I would **MARRY** you in a heartbeat," the bearded girl said.

Ewww!

Okay, yeah, I did consider it.

Don't judge. . .I've been kinda lonely lately, you know. . .

We were able to sneak into the cave without being detected.

And we waited until the Red Pumpkin had to tinkle.

TINKLE. . .tee, hee.

Now the only one that was guarding the Emerald was the Red Pumpkin's cat, which didn't seem like a problem.

"Hey, this is our chance," I said. "It's only the cat up there."

So, me and Laslow made it all the way to the top, where the altar was.

Then we quietly snuck behind the Emerald so we wouldn't wake up the cat.

The Emerald was stuck in a big hole in the wall, so we needed to push it out.

I squirmed in the hole behind the Emerald, and Laslow stood outside.

"Okay, Laslow, let's push on three. One. . .two. . .three. . .push!"

We tried to move it, but it just wouldn't budge.

"One. . .two. . .three. . .**PUSH!**"

Nothing.

"One. . .two. . .three. . .push!"

Still nothing.

Then, we decided to take a break.

"Man, that's really hard," I said. "I'm not sure how we're going to get that Emerald out of that hole."

"Out of hole? I thought you were telling me to push it in the hole."

Well, once we got coordinated, the Emerald started moving pretty easily.

Suddenly, we heard,

"MEOOOOOOWWW!"

Next thing I know, the cat stepped on a button on the throne and the Emerald started glowing.

All of a sudden, Laslow's eyes started shining with a green glow.

Then he started yelling and pointing in my direction.

"MEEP, MEEP, MEEP!"

"Shhh! Laslow keep quiet," I whispered.

And then my BEARD fell off.

Suddenly, the whole place went crazy. The eyes of every gnome in the place glowed green, and they all started yelling.

"MEEP, MEEP, MEEP!"

So, I ran out of the cave as fast as I could.

But then I ran into the rest of the gnome gang outside.

"MEEP, MEEP, MEEP!"

They all tried grabbed me. But it was a good thing that they were puny because I shook them off like a buck-toothed tick.

Then, I got out of there as fast as I could.

TUESDAY

I tried to tell my mom and dad about the Red Pumpkin and the gnomes this morning, but they thought I was still trying to make **EXCUSES** about my essay so they didn't believe me.

So, I turned on our new TV to show them all the carnage the gnomes were causing all over the town.

But there was nothing.

I went to every channel, and nobody was talking about anything.

"Zombie, please stop making up **STORIES,**" my mom said.

"Zombie, remember. . .with great power comes great responsibility," my dad said.

Yeah, dads say some of the weirdest things sometimes.

But then it hit me.

I bet Laslow played another practical joke on me!

URRRRRGGGHHHH! That little booger got me again!

I could imagine him laughing right now.

Tee hee hee.

My mom and dad took Wesley to his school while I stayed home.

I was grounded for trying to make up stories in order not to do my homework.

So I just tried watching some TV, to take my mind off how **MAD** I was.

So much for the Red Pumpkin unleashing his fury, I thought.

But then, all of a sudden I heard. . .

Gnomes, Gnomes. . .Get your gnomes, get your gnomes, get your gnomes.

Gnomes, Gnomes. . .Get your gnomes at the Red Pumpkin!

Get your Gnome and get good luck, get good luck, get good luck.

Get your Gnome and get good luck at the Red Pumpkin!

Then the Red Pumpkin came out on the TV and with his creepy voice he said. . .

"Well, it's that time boys and girls. It's time for you to destroy! It's time for you to demolish! It's time for you to plunder! It's time for you to unleash my fury on all of Minecraft!"

"MUAHAHAHAHAHAHA!"

Next thing I know, a giant red pumpkin starts to flash on and off on the screen, over and over again.

And after a while, I started to feel like I was going to hurl.

Suddenly, I heard screaming and breaking and **MANIACAL** laughing outside.

So I ran to the window.

I saw the house next door burst into flames.

And then the house down the street exploded in front of my eyes.

I saw mobs of my neighbors screaming and running for their lives with little gnomes grabbing at their heads.

Then I saw gnomes carrying entire mob families away.

The TV kept **FLASHING** the red pumpkin over and over, faster and faster.

I kept getting weaker and weaker, until suddenly, I couldn't move.

I mean, I was totally frozen and I couldn't even move a muscle.

The remote was on my lap, but I couldn't reach it. So I just kept trying to lean forward as far as I could.

FLUMP!

Luckily, my hard head changed the channel.

On the next channel, the news was reporting about all the **CARNAGE** that was happening all around our village.

Then, suddenly, the Red pumpkin started flashing on the TV again.

So, I changed the channel quick. But it was playing on every channel!

I was frozen again, except now I didn't have the remote.

I was fading, and everything was turning black.

I could see the shadows of little creatures as they approached behind me.

All I could do was sit there and DROOL.

This is it! I thought.

This is the end.

WEDNESDAY

"Zombie. . ."

"Zombie. . ."

"ZOMBIE!"

"Urrrgghhhh. . .huhwuzzat?"

When I opened my eyes, Alex was hovering over my corpse.

"Zombie, are you okay?" Alex asked.

"What happened? I thought I was a GONNER for sure."

"You almost were," she said. "You're lucky I was on my way to your house this morning. I needed a dummy for my sword practice."

"Hey!"

"But, Alex, did you feel it?" I asked. "I mean, I couldn't move. It felt like my whole body was a **POPSICLE.**"

"Actually, I didn't," Alex said. "For some reason, I was fine."

That's weird, I thought. It's the same thing that happened in the cafeteria.

But then I thought, *Oh, man, the village!*

"Alex, how's the village? Is everybody okay?"

"Zombie. . .I'm sorry, but there's no village left."

"What?!!"

Oh, man, this is terrible.

But then I realized, **MY PARENTS!**

"Alex, how about my parents? Did they make it out?"

Alex didn't know what to say. I think it was because she really didn't know.

As I sat there thinking about my parents and my little brother, Wesley, I started to tear up.

"There, there, Zombie. It's going to be all right," I heard Alex say as she patted me with her baby hands.

Wait. . . **BABY HANDS?!!!!**

Then I looked up, and Laslow was standing next to me patting me on the head.

"Laslow!"

I grabbed the little gnome, turned him upside down, and started **SHAKING** him.

He was kicking and screaming, and trying to say something but I didn't care. I wasn't going to let him trick me again.

Then I pinned him down on the ground and prepared to do my Ultimate Warrior Body Slam Super Elbow Dropkick on him.

"Calm down, Zombie," Alex said. "Laslow helped me get you out of there."

"What?!! Him?!!"

"Yeah, he helped me hide you in this cave when all of the gnomes took the mob villagers away."

"Zombie, I know you're mad at me," Laslow said. "And, I don't blame you. But I know where your parents are, and your friends."

"Well, you better start talking or you'd better get ready to rumble."

Then Laslow told me how the gnomes KIDNAPPED all the villagers and took them back to the Red Pumpkin's lair.

"Zombie, I think you know what we need to do." Alex said as she strapped on her bow and her sword.

Man, Alex is so tough for a human girl.

She reminds me of Lara Craft, the **TOMBRAIDER.**

It's kind of hot, in a creepy human way.

"Well, if we're going to rescue everybody," I said, "then we need to destroy the Mind Emerald once and for all. That's the source of the Red Pumpkin's power."

"Sounds like a plan," Alex said.

"But this time, Laslow," I said, "you're staying here. We don't need you having another meltdown."

"I have the perfect solution for that," Laslow said, showing me his big **HAIRY EARS.** "Worked like a charm yesterday."

Eh, I didn't have the energy to argue, so I let Laslow tag along.

Plus, I felt kinda jealous.

Those are some really big ears.

"Let's wait till dark," Alex said. "That way we can sneak up on them."

"Sounds like a plan," I said.

"Sounds like a plan."

☀ THURSDAY ☀

When we reached the Red Pumpkin's lair, they had all the villagers tied up, and they were leading them up to the Mind Emerald.

They had all the Creepers, Zombies, Skeletons, and Enderman tied up in minecarts so they couldn't get away.

"What are they doing with all the villagers?" Alex asked.

"They are going to be turned into **MINDLESS** zombies," Laslow said.

I just gave him a dirty look.

Then I told them, "The Mind Emerald only controls Minecraft mobs. That's probably why it doesn't affect you, Alex."

"But what does the Red Pumpkin need a bunch of **HYPNOTIZED** mobs for?"

"He is building an army to take over all of Minecraft," Laslow said.

Me and Alex just looked at each other.

"Whoa!"

While we were putting together our **RESCUE** plan, we didn't notice the cat that came strolling into our hiding spot.

"Whose cat is that?" Alex asked.

"RUN!" I yelled.

"MEEEOOOOOWWWWW!!!"

Then all the gnomes and hypnotized mobs came rushing at us.

"MEEP, MEEP, MEEP!"

But, there were too many of them. They caught us and put us in **CHAINS.** Then they led us to a dungeon deep inside the cave, and they threw us in and locked the door.

"What are we going to do?" Laslow stuttered. "I'm too young to die."

"Young? How old are you?" I asked, looking at his beard.

"Oh, I'm only twelve years old," he said, smiling.

"But what about that beard?"

"Oh, we're born like this," he said. "But we usually have a lot more **HAIR**. Especially the women."

I had too much on my mind to try to figure that one out.

So nasty.

✳ THURSDAY ✳
LATER THAT NIGHT. . .

We were in that dungeon for a few hours.

Then, suddenly, the big dungeon door swung open and Franklin the Enderman walked in.

Oh, man, I couldn't believe I would say this but I was really glad to see him.

Except Franklin was acting kind of weird. His eyes were green, and he was in some sort of a **TRANCE.**

"Franklin, you okay, buddy?" I asked him.

Then he grabbed us.

"BAMF!"

Next thing I know, Franklin teleported us to the **ALTAR,** in front of the Red Pumpkin and the Mind Emerald.

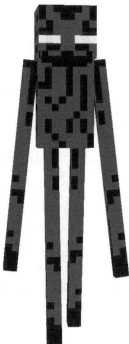

"MUE, HE, HE, HE, Heh," the Red Pumpkin said in his creepy voice, while stroking his cat.

"So, you thought you were going to **STOP** me from unleashing my fury on your village, heh?"

"You're not going to get away with this!" Laslow said to the Red Pumpkin.

Then Franklin picked up Laslow by his leg and began to **SHAKE** him until he got all dizzy.

Then Franklin stepped toward Alex.

"You want to try that with me, you overgrown blockhead?" Alex said in her Lara Craft voice.

Like I said. . .so **HOT.**

Then Franklin backed off.

"MUE, HE, HE, HE, Heh," the Red Pumpkin laughed in his creepy voice again.

"So, if it isn't Alex," the Red Pumpkin continued. "I could use someone like you to lead my legions into battle. Why don't you join me in my reign of terror? MUEH, HE, HE, HE, Heh!"

"I will never join you," Alex said. "Especially with that lame laugh. . .so **CLICHÉ.**"

"Oh, I think I can persuade you," the Red Pumpkin said, looking weirdly at me.

Then Franklin grabbed me by the neck.

"GACK!"

Suddenly, the Red Pumpkin started monologuing. . .

"It's about time we ended Minecraft and all of the destruction it has caused in the human world. No longer will human kids be obsessed over the game. No longer will children find it difficult to stay focused in school. And no longer will Minecraft turn human kids into **MINDLESS** zombies who have no social life."

"Hey!" I said as Franklin grabbed tighter.

"GACK!"

The Red Pumpkin continued, "But today, I will remake Minecraft in a mom's image!"

"Wait. . .what?"

"From now on, Minecraft will only teach kids math, and English, and history, and science!"

Oh no, this can't be happening.

"And there will be a **TIME LIMIT** of two hours per day of Minecraft screen time!"

No, no, no, no!

"And there will be no more **FIGHTING** over who is going to play first. No more fighting about problems on the server. No more whining about somebody trolling your build. No more wasting time trying to find a server without bad words!"

I can't believe this!

"I am going to reshape Minecraft so that it's approved by mom's everywhere!"

"MUAHAHAHAHA!"

"NNOOOOOOOOOO!!!!!!" I couldn't take his blasphemy any longer. He was going to take our beloved video game and turn it into a wasteland of kid appropriate play and **EDUCATIONAL** content.

I had to stop it, even if my life depended on it!

So, I lunged at the Red Pumpkin with all my strength and grabbed onto his big pumpkin head.

Franklin the Enderman tried to pry me off, but not before I took off the Red Pumpkin's big head.

Then everybody gasped.

"Cassie!" Alex yelled.

"Yes, it's me, Alex! And you remember Oslow," she said as the unmasked cat jumped on the altar.

"MEEEOOOOWWWW!"

"But Cassie, why?" Alex asked. "Why would you do such a thing? Why would you **DESTROY** Minecraft and ruin the fun that it brings to millions of kids all around the world? Why would you destroy all the meaningless escape it brings to the lives of kids everywhere?"

"Why? Because my name is not really Cassie. My name is Mabel. Mabel Mombottom!"

"Huh!"

"And I am a MOM of three preteen kids!"

"Huh!"

"And I got sick and tired of all the drama that MINECRAFT brought to my life, and to the lives of countless other moms in the human world!" Mabel continued. "So I stole both parts of the Mind Emerald, and now combined, I am going to use it to unleash my fury on all of Minecraft!"

"MUAHAHAHAHA!"

While Mabel dragged on, I used the opportunity to put on the Red Pumpkin head. It made it really easy to sneak away from Franklin the Enderman.

Then I found Laslow, and we both snuck behind the Mind Emerald.

"This is it Laslow, are you ready to finally **DESTROY** this thing?" I said.

"Ready!"

Then we both pushed with all our might.

Suddenly, the Mind Emerald tumbled off the altar and down to the rocks in the cave below.

"KRESH!"

WHAT HAVE YOU DONE?!!!! Mabel Mombottom said.

All of a sudden, a giant **VORTEX** formed and it started sucking what looked like green ooze out of the eyes of all of mobs and all the gnomes.

Then Mabel and Oslow ran toward the Mind Emerald. But as they got closer, they started getting sucked into the vortex too.

"NO! NO! NO! NOOOOOOOOOOO!"

Then as it **SUCKED** them into the vortex, Mabel said the scariest words I would ever hear my entire life. . .

"ONE DAY MINECRAFT WILL BE MOM FRIENDLY! I PROMISE YOU! I PROMISE YOOOOOOOOU!!!!!!!!

Then the vortex closed, and everything got quiet.

Then suddenly, the whole cave erupted with cheers.

"YEAAAAAAHHHHH!!!!!"

Everybody started cheering and hugging and jumping and teleporting and hissing.

Then all the gnomes came out and were welcomed with open arms by all the Minecraft mob villagers.

And they all lived happily ever after.

Yeah right. . .

Actually, the mob villagers were still a little **FREAKED OUT** by the creepy looking gnomes coming to life.

And they weren't too happy that the gnomes destroyed our village.

But Laslow jumped in and PROMISED that he and his gnome companions were going to fix the village all up again.

And so that made things a little better.

But I don't think we're going to be having any gnomes over for dinner anytime soon.

FRIDAY

Well, the gnomes started
REBUILDING our village today.

Except, I don't think it's going to look
like it did before.

I think maybe it was the round doors
and the mushroom house tops.

But I guess it's okay.

And I totally didn't mind the big green
pipes in the middle of the street.

The good thing is that my mom and dad, and my little brother Wesley are back **SAFE** at home.

I was really worried because I thought the Red Pumpkin got them.

But I found out later that the gnomes left Wesley's school alone.

I heard they were overwhelmed by the

destructive might of the Pre-school
Chicken jockeys.

Franklin didn't remember anything
that happened.

He even called me today and said he
wanted me to come over.

He said he wanted me to come over
and play his **FAVORITE** game, find
my belly button.

Yeah, I let it go to voicemail.

But you know, I still get the creeps
every time I remember Mabel's last
words.

"MINECRAFT WILL BE MOM
FRIENDLY ONE DAY!"

Whreewwww. Gives me shivers every time I think about it.

The whole episode didn't scare Alex away, though.

She decided to stay in my school, even after everything that happened with crazy Mabel.

Yeah, Alex is one cool girl.

And I know what you're thinking.

But I don't think I should go there.

That's because there's a crazy **PROPHECY** that said if a human and Zombie ever got married, then it would mean the end of the world as we know it.

And I'm trying to reduce the drama in my life, remember?

But you know, even though I can add this whole episode to the long list of drama in my life. . .

I think I'm okay with it now.

Yeah, my life is crazy, bonkers with a whole lot of weird and a few nuts thrown in.

But, you know, it kinda makes my life way more **INTERESTING.**

And compared to living a boring zombie preteen life, I think I'm okay with a little drama in my life. . .

. . .once in a while.

FIND OUT WHAT HAPPENS NEXT!

DIARY OF A
MINECRAFT ZOMBIE

BOOK 16

DOWN
THE
DRAIN

ZACK
ZOMBIE

AN UNOFFICIAL MINECRAFT BOOK

DOWN THE DRAIN

Zombie's village has gone through some **major changes**. And **two strange looking sewer workers** have been snooping around looking for a **princess they lost**.

Join Zombie and his friends as they take a trip "Down the Drain" to help these two goofballs **RESCUE THEIR PRINCESS FROM A NEW AND INFAMOUS VILLAIN.**

CPSIA information can be obtained
at www.ICGtesting.com
Printed in the USA
LVHW081737010522
717657LV00006B/173

9 781943 330881